These stories first appeared, sometimes in slightly different form, in the following magazines:

Apricity, "The Strange Case of Patient C"
Black Scat Review, "Closing Credits in the Culture Wars" and "Laurel and Hardy Have Sex"
BlazeVOX, "Here Lies a Myriad"
Burningwood Literary Journal, "The Prison Forecast"
Calibanonline, "Story Problem" and "Kickstart Me Harder, Harder"
Chaleur, "Love Kit"
EAP: The Magazine, "Second Thoughts" and "The Exterminating Clarity of the Coffee Shop"
Journal of Compressed Creative Arts, "Annals of Contemporary Gastronomy"
Lowestoft Chronicle, "Quality Time Over the Holidays"
Medulla Review, "For Better For Worse"
North American Review, "Letter of Rec" and "Story of Ralph"
Sisyphus, "The Pain of Patriotic Dysfunction"

"But have I fall'n, or no?"

King Lear, IV.6

Contents

AGITPROP
FOR
BEDTIME

Polemic, Story Problems,
Kulturporn and Humdingers

CHARLES
HOLDEFER

Set in Mrs Eaves XLwith LaTeX.

ISBN: 978-1-944697-99-0 (paperback)
ISBN: 978-1-952386-00-8 (ebook)
Library of Congress Control Number: 2020933760

Sagging Meniscus Press
Montclair, New Jersey
saggingmeniscus.com

AGITPROP

FOR

BEDTIME

The Pain of Patriotic Dysfunction: One Man's Testimony

This subject is embarrassing but that's why I step forward, with my personal account, so that any guy out there with a similar problem will know: *you are not alone.*

I'll be blunt: I used to stand for the national anthem with my hand over my heart and a bulging erection in my pants. Yes, I'm a patriotic fellow, I make no apology. Passion is its own master.

I admit to being perplexed, in my younger days, to comments about my responsiveness. (I don't say this out of vanity but my patriotism did attract some notice.) It was simply a spontaneous reaction. I liked the anthem! At "dawn's early light" I was snaking out and emerging. By "rockets' red glare," my aspirations were decidedly skyward.

Honestly, I didn't bother to think about *why*. It just felt natural.

But lately something unwelcome has happened. Or, to be more accurate, has *not* happened. Why is that? Honestly, it pains my psyche.

Why don't I get an immediate erection when I hear the national anthem?

I also wonder if there are other patriotic American males experiencing the same dysfunction. The effect is disorienting. Upsetting. No doubt they're asking the same question.

What accounts for the change?

A delicate subject, to be sure. And, while I don't pretend to know the answers, I would like to offer some preliminary observations.

First—and please remember that I'm not trying to make excuses or assign blame, OK?—I'd be less than honest if I didn't mention an aspect of the situation which is hard to shake from my mind. It's this: America doesn't appear as beautiful as it used to be.

I'm just going to put that out there.

Second, I acknowledge that it's a two-way street! *Of course*. People might say that I'm not so hot myself, as an American citizen. Maybe I've let myself go? Taken too much for granted? I admit that this might be true, too.

Nobody's perfect, but nobody needs to be hurt here, all right?

I wonder if this problem affects many mature relationships. What used to be so obvious and effortless now requires attention.

Short cuts are tempting, but they don't offer long-term satisfaction. For instance, I've gotten through a few anthems by fantasizing about Norway. I don't deny it.

It wouldn't surprise me if there are other red-blooded fellows out there resorting to similar psychological tricks. Priming themselves before a game by privately watching videos of Trondheim recycling centers or deepwater fjords.

It is not for me to judge.

Still, such tricks avoid confronting the origin of the problem and they don't offer long-term satisfaction. Because it's America that I love! Whereas Norway—well, it looks fabulous, sure, how can you be blind to such charms? (I'm one of those people who likes it clean.) But Norway isn't home and never will be.

Others turn to prescription medicine. It can help a person to make it through the song. I won't criticize them. That is their choice, and it can answer a need.

But I know what's right for me, and in my heart I doubt that medicating myself is the best way to get through our national sing-along. Call me romantic. I don't care! A chemical will not serve as the solution to the underlying issues of a relationship.

Because that's what this is about. A lasting relationship. I'm in this for the long haul.

That's where it stands with me.

Or doesn't stand.

The point is, we need to talk.

Annals of Contemporary Gastronomy: American Soul Food

Commonly considered a folk favorite but also savored by a slice of urban elite and, more recently, by a new style of religiously-minded devotee, this dish is typically consumed fresh and steaming hot and sometimes more than once in a day, courtesy of the President of the United States, since it comes directly out of his ass.

For many it is delivered more quickly than pizza into the privacy of their homes, packaged in surprising—yet characteristically incontinent—spellings. On other occasions it is served in public venues like racetracks or stadiums in the presence of hungry, eager crowds. Whatever the numbers in attendance, people share a common meal, à la loaves and fishes.

Is it good for you? Or quite the opposite? Is it merely a nostalgic *frisson* or a taste of the future? Is it foul or authentic, or authentic because it is foul?

These questions are sources of debate, especially among Americans who dislike it. But even critics appear to become habituated and capable of consuming larger and larger doses, thereby adding to its ubiquity.

Whether you are an aficionado or a detractor, it is a fact that this dish is impossible to avoid. And this raises another, oft-discussed practical matter. Can you consume it without getting some of it on you?

Or is that OK, like barbecue?

Amid today's concerns about the obesity epidemic, type 2 diabetes, LDL cholesterol and compromised gut flora—all worthy subjects—and the debates about local versus imported, and questions of purity—also very timely—it is necessary to keep in mind the larger picture, too.

What are the dietary consequences of this dish, in its peculiar nourishment of the American soul?

Story Problem

A fat man in his underwear stands on a diving board. Behind him, pines climb the air beyond a chain-link fence. The swimming pool is designed to hold a maximum of 400,000 liters of water. The volume of evaporation on a spring day—just like today—is .0008 liters per hour at 17° Celsius. A woman walks away from the pool, ignoring his calls. He insists that these pleas are his story, but she doesn't know what to believe, a fact that breaks her heart. The man weighs 94 kilos and, if he executes a perfect belly-smacker into 400,000 liters, his body mass could displace as much as six liters of water into the air. Such a tremendous splash! The glitter of droplets would linger in *your* eye after the sound of impact while the breeze carried the delighted cries of a child who also witnessed the dive.

But no one is watching today. In the upstairs apartment overlooking the swimming pool, a television commercial sings *"Up, up and away!"* as a child unscrews the lid on a jar of peanut butter and prepares to scrape together another sandwich. When the pool is full, a person standing on the diving board can see the reflection of overflying birds en route to unknown destinations.

Today the pool is not full. It is empty. The man watches the woman disappear into the building to begin a new story which will not include him. The child does not know this yet but is very hungry. The man jumps. The last thing he notices is the brown spot of the drain, rushing toward him. Did the pines hear his impact? Why is there so much unhappiness?

Second Thoughts

When the doorbell rang, Wayne stopped buffing and polishing and went to answer.

"Oh, it's you."

"Hello. I believe you know why I'm here."

"Are you sure it's necessary?"

"Honey, who is it?" Courtney called from the kitchen.

Wayne yelled over his shoulder. "It's Nancy Pelosi. She's come to take our guns." He turned back to the Majority Leader. "I guess I'd better let you in. But I'm not happy about this."

"I won't be long."

Wayne's Ruger Redhawk lay on the coffee table, gleaming next to the summer issue of *House Beautiful*.

"Well, we can start with that one."

Pelosi snapped open a pillow case.

"I didn't hear you." Courtney entered the room with a fresh mug of coffee. "Oh . . . I see."

Pelosi eyed the rifle above the fireplace.

"That was grandpa's .22," Wayne explained. "His dad gave it to him when he was twelve years old. Used it for squirrels, mainly, and to develop his aim. He gave it to my dad, who later gave it to me. I've been saving it for my grandchildren. That gun has been in the family since the nineteenth century."

The Congresswoman looked around. "Dianne!" she called. "Got another one for you."

Senator Feinstein came rattling into the living room with a little red wagon.

"Huh? What?"

Pelosi pointed.

"Right, Nance. I'm on it."

Feinstein trotted around the couch and reached above the fireplace and began to grapple with the gun.

"You got anything else for me?" Pelosi asked. "Shotguns? Semi-automatics? Hollow-point bullets and armor-piercing cartridges? Bump stocks? We sure appreciate it when citizens hand them in, I want you to know that."

"Geez," Feinstein puffed. "What's with this thing?"

"Just a sec." Wayne moved to help her. "It tends to stick."

Courtney excused herself and soon returned with a snub-nosed revolver. "Here's our .357 from the night stand." Pelosi opened her pillow case. Next Courtney retrieved her purse and, after rooting around, came up with a tiny nickel-plated Beretta 9000. "This was my Christmas present." She dropped it in, too.

"Any long guns?" Pelosi pursued.

"Those are locked up in the basement," said Wayne. "We're responsible owners."

"Could you get them, please?"

Feinstein lay the .22 rifle to rest in her wagon and smiled in satisfaction as they listened to Wayne pound down the basement steps; presently they heard him slowly pounding his way back up. He arrived with his arms laden. "There are only these four. The kids took the others when they went to college."

The guns tumbled into the wagon.

"Thank you," said Pelosi. "We won't trouble you anymore." She twisted the top of the pillow case but before she knotted it, she looked back and forth between Wayne and Courtney. "Listen. You sure you're not forgetting any? Give it a think."

Wayne and Courtney were silent at first. Eventually Wayne blurted, "Oh, my goodness! Now that you mention it, there *is* one in the kitchen. Doggone!" Courtney sighed as he left them and moments later he returned with a box of cornflakes. He removed a .45 AMT Hardballer.

"Well well," said Feinstein. "That's some prize in your cereal!"

"If you want to know the truth," said Courtney, "we hid it there in anticipation of a day when we might have to take our country back. But never mind. It's too late now."

The Hardballer dropped into the pillow case.

"Don't worry, folks." Pelosi slung the bag over her shoulder. "*Ho ho ho!*"

The Congresswoman and Senator walked out the front door, and Wayne and Courtney fell into each other's arms, their hearts beating fast as they listened to the squeak of wagon wheels growing fainter in the distance.

"I guess we always knew this would happen," she said.

"It's not our fault," he said.

He pulled down the blinds and they sat on the couch. For several minutes, they faced the windows in silence. What now? What was left? A tightness welled up in Wayne's chest, and suddenly he clenched his fists and wailed, "I feel so infringed!"

Sobs shook him, and though Courtney reached out, she could not make him stop.

Reckoning

Sorry to see our unicorn approach the bolt. But it had lost its teeth, it was lame from hoof-rot. Its mane shed stringy wisps.

Worst of all was the Horn, which I tried to reattach when it fell off. Oh, I tried so hard!

But now it was crooked. Rolling its eyes, the Poor Beast lunged after the point, bleating. Raging. Mad. What else could I do?

There comes a time for taking stock.

Making sense.

Glue.

The Strange Case of Patient C

Patient C insisted that she should have "access" (*sic*) to health care. She used this term repeatedly, and it emerged as the primary symptom of her condition.

A generous grant from Freedom Street® allowed us to conduct several interviews with the subject. We hoped to find a diagnosis and a therapeutic option to help Patient C on her healing journey.

As a first step, she was referred to a lexicologist.

Report 1.1

Confidential

Repeated attempts were made to persuade Patient C that "access" in the sense she assumed did not exist for everyone. She appeared to be suffering from a definition deficit. Side effects included perplexity and incomprehension.

Despite our efforts, Patient C did not relent. Her condition aggravated to the extent that she argued for a "right" and asserted it was "universal." Her preoccupation with "access" had reached an advanced stage.

After a prolonged interview, it became obvious that Patient C was not responding to clarification. Her symptom was too deeply rooted.

She was referred to an etymologist.

Report 1.2

Confidential

With a gentle preparation of the background, Patient C was informed that a "right" was a pre-existing condition. Moreover, a "right" was a proposition unavailable to scientific consensus and, even more troubling, the concept of "rights" was a common argument among market denialists.

Every effort was made not to accuse or morally judge the patient, but professional standards required that Patient C be informed of the problematic foundations of her assumptions.

Unfortunately, Patient C did not respond well to edifying treatment. She became visibly agitated. While still clinging to words like "access" and "universal," she began to emphasize other terms, too, such as "mercenary" and "asshole." She also displayed symptoms of shortness of breath and compromised aggressive impulse control, which brought an end to the consultation, as Patient C was escorted from the room with the help of several medical orderlies.

At this point, the record becomes less clear, given the lack of authorized professional observers, but it appears that Patient C did not leave the hospital but lingered in a waiting area, either by accident or provocation. Witnesses claim that she continued to insist on "access." According to the receptionist on duty, many people in the waiting area cried out similar statements, often in a state of heightened emotion.

Was Patient C's condition contagious? At present, this hypothesis remains uncorroborated. But anecdotal accounts do suggest that Patient C and numerous others resorted to the same words.

In an effort to defuse an alarming situation while probing more deeply into her incomprehension (e.g., was Patient C suffering from a failure of phonemes that had impeded her morphemes? had she lost control of her vowels?), the subject was offered an emergency consultation with a phonologist.

Report 2.1

Confidential

Initial observations were encouraging. In fact, Patient C seemed articulate and in command of her thoughts and speech. She was consistently understandable. Nonetheless, her primary symptom persisted: she showed no sign of abandoning her claim to "access."

Thus it would seem that the patient's clarity and rationality are asymptomatic.

Vital signs such as pulse and respiration were variable, depending on her interlocutor's degree of refusal.

Most worrying, however, were the following vitals: 1) the credit clearance of her Visa card was unsatisfactory; 2) her employment and insurance situation offered no plausible palliative. These findings were verified twice by the billing department.

Preliminary conclusion

Confidential

The case of Patient C remains inexplicable. At the time of this writing, she is languishing in a tautology ward. The prognosis is not good.

For Better For Worse

"Honey?"

"Yeah, what is it now?"

"When I crack up and hide under the sheets and my hair is mussed for all the world beyond the drapes and there's nothing but pain within you because you can't trust the face that I've put on for everyone else to see since I've betrayed you utterly, will you bring me grapes?"

Letter of Rec

Moses, Socrates, Jesus—and now Lorrie Carter. It is my great pleasure to inform whomever it may concern that Lorrie is one of the finest individuals ever to pass through our offices, a credit to our community, our state, our nation, our continent (before and after drift). Not only do I have the deepest respect for the incontestable quality of Laurie's work, I also feel compelled to add, for the record, that I *love* it—with more than a deeply heartfelt filial affection, with excitement more electric than any erotic surge, with what can only be described as Purest Esteem, we're talking 200 proof *agape*. Moreover, RAH! RAH! RAH! RAH! RAH! RAH! RAH!!!! How we shall continue after Laurie's departure tortures our souls, and it is only a measure of our indebtedness that mass suicide remains a distinct possibility. What bliss awaits the lucky ones who will next cross paths with this charismatic (and always punctual!) dynamo. Without reservation and with warmest regards, I recommend this stellar applicant: you can count on Larry.

Wes T. Manntase

The Prison Forecast

"Welcome, Tim!"

"Great to be on the show, Jill!"

"So—what's your outlook on today's prison market?"

"Well, I've been bullish for a long time, and the private sector has done well by any metric. All is solid on the fundamentals. The U.S. has the highest incarceration rate in the world. More than China, more than Russia. Belarus isn't even close. Cuba and Saudi Arabia can't touch us. The numbers don't lie. The smart investor can still hope to see a good return."

"But can growth continue? Some people say that opioids have created a bubble."

"Don't believe the doomsayers! You hear lots of sensational things in the media, but I don't think the market has peaked. Here's an inconvenient truth for the hand-wringers, Jill: opioids bring repeat customers. It's a very loyal base. We're seeing growth in rural America that folks wouldn't have dreamed of a few years ago. And that puts a premium on our product. Law enforcement needs us. And so do hard-working, law-abiding citizens. We're renewing a vital infrastructure and we're big job creators. Construction and security contractors, laundry services and independent catering—you name it. Forget the fancy talk. The hotel industry isn't seeing this kind of growth. Theme parks are saturated. But we're still expanding."

"How's that look from the inside? Break it down for me. What's hot and what's not?"

"It's a question of vision, of keeping up with changes in today's world. Some people hear the word "prison" and they think: rapists and murderers. Armed robbery. Arson. To their mind, that's the brand. OK, that's our legacy, sure, but in reality there's so much more—for instance, we're seeing an uptick in incarcerations of undocumented people. For a long time it was a sleeper sector, but lately we've been tapping an unrealized potential. There's less red tape involved, compared to regular prisoners, which brings a promising margin for the savvy provider. I'm bullish on the undocumented."

"How about juveniles?"

"Depends. Investors need to do their homework. Different states have different codes. Overall, though, progress is being made, because we're getting some leadership from the top. Nobody with skin in the game really wants bureaucratic meddling."

"Terrorism? Where does it fit into this cycle?"

"We're growing partnerships internationally, and domestically, we're probably going to see some movement. I don't have a crystal ball, but indicators suggest that we can expect more activity in this area. Nobody wants to think about it, but professionals in the field are rolling up their sleeves and they'll be ready. A big part of our value added is being poised so that the rest of America doesn't *have* to think about it. People sleep better at night knowing that the invisible hand has long arms. Count on us, Jill. We'll be there!"

"Thanks, Tim. We'll take a commercial break, and next up, exciting news for folks worried about the carbon footprint of electric chairs and gas chambers. Made of 100% recycled hemp, it's the environmentally-friendly noose!"

Love Kit

I.

"I wish they'd just put it into clear words. Jesus, all these images are confusing! Who can understand this stuff?"

"The instructions say it's supposed to be universal."

"What?"

"That way everybody can understand."

"You've got to be kidding."

II.

Does it fit?
Is this the right hole?
Are we happy?

III.

"It looked better in the catalog, the way you'd imagine it should be."

"I dunno. I half-expected this."

"Really?"

"Don't get mad. I mean, if it looks different for us now, maybe it's because of the surroundings. That could explain it."

"Right. It's not us."

IV.

Try it the other way around.

Or maybe this way?

You're standing in my light!

V.

"Fuck! Fuck! Fuck!"

"Oh, God—now it's damaged."

"You're blaming me? Is that what you're saying?"

"No, no, no."

"I'm so exasperated I could cry."

"It's a problem of design. That's what it is."

VI.

Or you could always just look the other way.

Or step around it.

Or over it.

Be frank—is it really hurting anything?

Don't expect too much.

VII.

"Say it's not true. How could you?"

"It's not what I wanted. I see that now."

"Then get the hell out! Go!"

"I'm so sorry. Goodbye."

RIGHT OF CANCELLATION *You may choose to do so at any time but there are no returns and no refunds, and you are responsible for additional costs.*

Here Lies a Myriad

"Hi, I'm Darrel and I'll be your server. Can I start you off with some fear, honor or disinformation?"

"Just water for now. We'll have a look at the menus."

As soon as he left them, she giggled and lifted the silverware, noticing the weight. "I've heard so much about this place!"

He looked around. "Everyone who works here is a hero. Every last one of them."

The interior hummed with vibrations from many rooms.

She opened her menu. "You know, my grandfather used to work here."

"Really? Mine, too!"

Darrel returned and poured ice water. He stood attentively at their side.

"We'll need a minute."

He clicked his heels and left them.

"I suppose it was different then," she said. "Back in the day, pretty much everybody served. It wasn't a professional outfit."

"Well, they might've been amateurs but their generation was the greatest."

"Yes," she agreed. "The greatest."

They fell silent as they perused the listings. It was hard to know where to begin. They'd heard the portions at this place were huge, but it seemed indelicate to say so. A busboy's cart whizzed by so fast that it made a sonic boom. Startled, they looked up, and Darrel stepped forward.

"May I take your orders?"

They weren't ready but he was poised and they felt obliged to tell him something. She quickly ran her finger down the menu. "I'll go with one of your specials. How about the psych ops?"

"Very good. It comes with cyber."

"That would be very nice, thank you."

Darrel turned. "And you, sir?"

"I'm sort of hesitating between a naval destroyer and the infantry."

Darrel leaned forward. "In that case, if you look a little further down, you'll see we offer surf and turf."

"Right. I'll try that."

"Might I suggest a starter of air strikes, to soften up your target?"

"Perfect!"

They were relieved when he left them—their decisions had been made—but in truth they weren't sure what to expect.

"Funny," he said. "You hear so much about this place but I've never seen it up close."

"I'd like to know what really goes on in the kitchen."

"Well, they have the latest equipment, the best in the world." He ran his hand across the blast-proof tablecloth. "That's what they say."

She shook open her napkin. "Don't you sometimes wonder how they treat their employees?"

"Darrel seems all right."

"True." She observed the female servers at nearby tables where birds circled overhead. "You have to admit, there's more diversity than at our workplace."

He nodded. Although he hadn't said it aloud, he'd noticed how Darrel was polite and well-spoken. Not a single grammar mistake.

For a moment they gazed fondly at each other and shared identical thoughts: no way would they choose to work *here*. It was hard even to imagine. Maybe as a chef in the kitchen—that could be interesting—but it wasn't an entry-level position and you would have to work your way up the ranks, which was tedious, all that travel and low pay, no thanks. This place might have a spit-and-polish presentation but behind it all was something unmistakably grubby. Real success waited elsewhere. Might as well leave this place to the folks who didn't know how to do better.

"I wonder," he offered slowly, "how many people here will get into substance abuse. Just saying."

"Tell me about it. Spousal abuse, too."

They nodded.

"That surely accounts for the divorce statistics. Off the charts!"

"And the children? Now that's harder to quantify, the price of unhappy, screwed-up kids, but the social cost is enormous."

"But everybody ends up paying for it. We're paying for it."

"Oh hell yes."

"Word."

They nodded.

Now she blurted: "Homelessness."

"Prisons!" he countered.

"Suicides!"

He hesitated, groping for another example to hold up his end of the dinner conversation. He cast his eyes around the room. Then it came to him.

"Some things," he murmured, "aren't on the menu. I heard that in season they do torture."

She frowned and looked away.

Instantly he regretted his words. Had he gone too far? Was that subject still supposed to be unmentionable? And then—oh my, what bad timing—a server in dress whites glided by, balancing a platter of purple hearts and scarred minds.

"Understand me," he added, "I mean no disrespect to all the good apples."

"Of course not."

There was another silence, readjusting their napkins on their laps while once more their thoughts were identical: images of tombstones like teeth protruding from immaculate green grounds and darting eyes of amputees and the intubated and the noseless and skin-grafted who watched the light change in the windows while waiting for visitors who didn't come, imploring: Will you change my diaper? Where is my morphine? Will someone come and change my diaper? Where are you? Why am I alone? What does it mean?

"Freshen that up for you?"

Darrel refilled their glasses, ice-cubes clinking.

They wished he wouldn't hover. Where were their orders? Damn, the kitchen was slow. And in Darrel's manner was something they hadn't noticed before, a weariness, or maybe an exasperation, as if he didn't like them.

But that was unfair. Why, he didn't even know them!

"We need to talk," she said softly.

He turned to Darrel. "Could you leave us for a minute?"

"Is there nothing else I can get you?"

"No. Thank you for your service."

Quality Time Over the Holidays

He'd drunk eleven pints. Now, with concentration, he pulled on his coat. Buttoning could come later. He ventured one foot. Then another. In the middle of the next step, he wondered: *Did I zip my fly?* He looked down and the floor came rushing up.

He fell with a crash.

"I'm OK!" he called.

He touched his knee and then his forehead. It seemed to be true.

He took a deep breath and rolled onto his back and tried to center himself before attempting to stand again.

A face loomed over him.

"Oh dear, look at you," his mother said softly. She touched his cheek. "You used to be such a sweet boy."

He squirmed. "Ma—come on. Hey! I'm trying to get up."

A bark of laughter startled him. He turned his head and saw his father on the floor beside him, lying on his back and grinning, his arms swimming toward the ceiling.

"Son!" he cried. "Chip off the old block!"

The Exterminating Clarity of the Coffee Shop

It should have been easy to leave the coffee shop. Sylvia finished her cup and headed to the cash register with its golden-lit display case of muffins as big as human brains. She looked around. Wasn't this the way she'd come in?

She tried going the other way, passing patrons who chatted over flat whites or fingered their phones. She discovered a small elevated stage and a pierced young man with a stand-up bass. He tested a string. *Plonk.* He smiled at her and shimmied his shoulders. *Plonk! Plonk!* Sylvia moved on.

Next to a potted ficus, a young mother tried to calm a fussy toddler who quivered in his stroller like he was on fire. Sylvia stepped around them and came to an area where the lighting was lower and group of young men with shaved heads and nail-studded bracelets shook sugar packets and debated about the best software for writing screenplays. Slowly, she backed away.

A woman in a green sweater stood up from her table, slung her purse over her shoulder and strode away purposefully. Sylvia decided to follow her. But the woman covered only a short distance before she entered a restroom.

Sylvia realized that she needed to go to the toilet, too, in no small part because of an encroaching anxiousness. She pressed into the restroom in time to see the door of the last stall closing. Sylvia chose the nearest stall and quickly sat down, telling herself: This is silly. As she peed, she gazed at the graffiti, a cartoon of stick people contorting in air, falling. It was like a cave painting by a Cro-Magnon with a Sharpie.

She didn't dawdle and after leaving the stall, she washed her hands and watched in the mirror. The last stall opened, the woman in green emerged. Sylvia lowered her eyes as she reached for a paper towel. She stole another glance: the woman was staring at her, her mouth slightly open as if out of breath.

"Excuse me," the woman said. "May I ask you a question?"

"Of course."

The woman busied herself at the tap. "It's frustrating," she continued, "but I came here this morning and, well, hard to explain, but maybe you can help me? I've been here a while and I need to leave. But somehow—" she shook her hands over the sink—"I can't seem to find the exit."

Sylvia laughed, but it was a nervous laugh, without mirth.

"I'm having the same problem."

"Oh." The woman gave a little sniff, reaching for a towel. "Well, this can't be all there is. Right? Maybe we can look together. I'm Angela."

Sylvia introduced herself and they left the restroom, passing a free-standing Art Deco lamp and an overstuffed chair where a white-haired man with half-moon reading glasses slowly turned the page of a newspaper, chuckling. Nearby, a couple bent over their cups and kissed.

"What about that way?" Angela said.

Beyond the lovers, they came upon a group of middle-aged women in pastel gym suits and bright leggings who consumed large lattes and cranberry scones while conversing about Pilates and dog obedience and carbs.

"Maybe over there?"

Sylvia pointed to a gap between piles of burlap bags of coffee beans. They slipped through and Angela remarked, "This looks familiar."

Sylvia observed the brick walls and also had the impression that she'd been here before. She became aware of a deep vibration, touching the base of her spine. It happened again, followed by a higher, plaintive note, a choked human voice.

"All those English schoolchildren
eating porridge out of skulls
believed their history was
THERE, pink on the map,
whole!"

They came around a corner and Sylvia recognized the raised stage, the young man with the stand-up bass. He bobbed his head and grasped at strings while a young woman in a black jumpsuit performed poetry.

"Today, a baby bursts!"

Sylvia grabbed Angela's arm and pulled her away, weaving between tables. *Plonk! Plonk!* They accelerated and dodged to the left, and then diagonally to the right, until they came to a carpeted space and Angela halted. "Look—over there."

On the wall, next to a framed Amish quilt, was a blue door. It wasn't marked as a restroom or fire exit. Sylvia went straight to it and tested the knob.

"It's not locked."

The door opened onto a narrow staircase, leading down.

"Come on!"

A thumping descent down wooden steps. At the bottom they found another door of gray metal with a large, horn-like handle. It wasn't locked, either, but it was heavy. Together they pushed and the door swung inward.

A scorching wave of air belched over them and they beheld a massive roaster that shivered and gleamed while a circle of sweating laborers shovelled beans into a slowly turning pan, the orbs of their caffeinated eyes bulging out of their streaked faces. In the distance, a mighty grinder roared. The atmosphere was dense with torrefaction, the air itself felt molten, viscous. Along the walls, an outer circle of workers frantically slathered pesto onto whole-grain bread.

Sylvia and Angela seized the handle and pulled the door closed. They ran back upstairs, a heavy aroma still clinging to their clothes.

"This way!"

"No, this way!"

They surged through an alcove and for a moment Sylvia's hopes soared, then she stopped short. It was the serving counter and cash register. The display case of muffins, bathed in golden light. A kid in an apron stood behind the register.

"Can I help you?" he asked. "Today, order one extra shot, get the second one free!"

"I don't want anything," Sylvia said. "Where's the exit, please?"

"Oh, that's not here. Would you like to place an order?"

Angela knelt in front of the display case. "I can see light on the other side." She tapped on the glass and tested the corners with her fingernails.

"Please," said the kid. "Don't serve yourself. We can help you."

"Will you answer my question?" Sylvia asked.

The glass slid to the floor with a crash.

"Dammit!" said Angela. "Sorry."

The kid was aghast. "I'm gonna call the manager."

Angela threw down her purse and started to climb into the case of muffins. A flush rose up Sylvia's neck, a spontaneous discomfort at an unimagined possibility. "*Hey!*" She knelt and reached after Angela. "Don't do that."

Angela rolled away and began kicking at the other side. There was another crash. "Yes!" she cried. "Yes! Come on."

A gust of cool air licked at Sylvia's face. She was aware of shouts behind her as she leaned forward to see. There wasn't really time to think when Angela grabbed her wrist and pulled.

"Just roll!" Angela shouted. "Roll!"

Moments later, she was falling.

She landed on a patch of dirt. She hit hard, though broken muffins helped to cushion her fall.

"You OK?" said Angela.

Sylvia nodded and tried to get up. Clay stuck to her knees, weeds poked at her hands. Angela steadied her till she found her feet.

The air was briny and chill. A gray sky hinted at rain. There was a sound of a siren, coming closer.

Without a word they moved on, hurrying on a dirt path littered with broken shells. They passed a circle of children who kicked at a smudged ball, or maybe it was a stunned furry animal. A boy paused for a moment to watch them, his mouth crooked, then he looked down and resumed his play.

They came to a field of cabbages, increasing their speed among the round, silent heads, and Sylvia wiped her hand across her chin and laughed, loving her deliverance but wondering how long it would last.

Kickstart Me Harder, Harder

Friends!

We need your support for our sustainably subversive operations which tax-deductibly stick it to the man.

Our commitment to artistic freedom depends entirely on somebody else's money.

Please mark the appropriate box(es) corresponding to your gifting preference. (You may choose several!) *Invest in your conscience!* THANK YOU!

☐ Yes I care! I will contribute $5 for every mile you walk in someone else's flip-flops—*sans* earbuds!

☐ Yes I care! I will contribute $50 for every page of your personal memoir manuscript that you can fold into a piece of erotic origami.

☐ Yes I care! I will contribute $100 for every time you look over your shoulder and ask, "Does my soul look big?"

Do you want to join our select circle of favored supporters? Do you really meme it? Consider the pledge options below, which also include complimentary gifts!

☐ Feel the love! I wanna meme your brains out baby at the **silver echelon** and I will contribute $500 if you perform a classic Bojangles tap sequence with two flying swing outs while in a voting booth.*

(*Complimentary free subscription to our mailing list included!)

☐ Feel the love! I wanna meme your brains out baby at the **gold echelon** and I will contribute $1000 if you spend the night in the high mountain nest of a giant raptor and its baby chicks.*

(*Complimentary DVD included!)

☐ Feel the love! I wanna meme your brains out baby at the **platinum echelon** and I will contribute $5000 if you refrain from ever again being hipper-than-thou.*

(*Complimentary plain white T-shirt included: please specify XS, S, M, L, XL, XXL, XXXL or un-stitched swaddling.)

And while you're at it . . .

☐ Kickstart me harder, harder! Make my donation monthly. God bless us, everyone!

Closing Credits in the Culture Wars

Take One:

Postmodernists in Love

"Darling, I can't fight it anymore."

She swallowed deeply.

"Truly, I feel so much . . ." She lifted her fingers and scratched quotation marks into the air: "*'love.'*"

His breaths came faster.

"Oh, baby, are you sure that's what you . . ." He lifted his fingers and scratched back: "*'mean?'*"

She nodded and they reached out, their fingers entwined as they gazed into each other's eyes, speechless.

Take Two:

Constitutional Originalists in Love

"Honey, darn it anyway, there's something that's got to be said."

He drew up his shoulders.

"What?" she asked. "Go ahead. And I don't care if it's not politically correct. Shoot!"

"I love you. Hear me? That's the straight talk and I stand my ground. And now I'm going to kiss you."

She leaned toward him.

"Yes, do! Our founding fathers were great kissers."

Take Three:

Woke Folk in Love

"Do you have something to tell me?" she asked.

He smiled as he rubbed her back. "Actually, I do."

"No, wait. Let me guess."

"Sure," he said, reaching for more oil. "I'm right here. I'm listening."

"You love me, don't you? Without preconceptions or non-reciprocal expectations. That's it, right?"

He sighed. "I couldn't have put it better myself."

Take Four:

Dudes in Love

"Babe, something's gotta be said."

"Wait," she told him. "First turn your cap backwards. Will you do that for me? It makes you so handsome."

He reached up and gripped the bill and re-adjusted it. She pressed her hands together and cooed.

"Here it is," he said. "I frickin' I love you."

"Oh, awesome!"

"I can't take my eyes off you."

She looked down at her shirt. "You like them?"

Take Five:

Nation Builders in Love

"Listen up, sweetie. Got something to say. But don't take it wrong." He sighed. "Sometimes I'm misunderstood."

"*¿Qué?*"

"It's like this. I love you, see?"

"*¡Qué!*"

"But I need to tie you up when we do it."

"*¿Por qué?*"

"That's how I like it. The way I express myself is manifest and cannot be abridged. Now give me your wrists."

Story of Ralph

One Monday night Ralph had an idea: he got up and turned off the football game, opened his laptop and wrote a story. He'd never been seized by such an urge before but he didn't hold back, and typed non-stop for a whole hour. "What are you doing?" his wife asked. "Quiet!" he said, "I'm writing a story." When he was finished she inquired: "What kind of story?" Ralph blinked in wonder. "A humdinger!" He clicked *save* and attached the document to an email and sent it to a magazine with a geographical place name. The next morning he received a reply of gratitude from an editor who said this story was without a doubt—in his humble, perceptive, very important opinion—a real humdinger, adding that he was sending a check for $5000 and he was sorry it couldn't be more. Ralph felt so pleased upon reading this that he called in sick at work, which was a good thing, for the doorbell rang at noon when he was struggling to open the plastic wrap on some ramen noodles and while he shook hands with the agent who explained that she charged only 15 per cent the phone jingled and the man on the other end wanted a hardback deal, about which poor Ralph didn't know what to say, actually had no opinion, but the agent took the phone and by the time she hung up the deal was struck at 400 (smackers, big fat Ks, Ralph told himself, hardly believing) so he accepted her offer of services and sat down, extremely pleased with himself, and made her open the noodles.

On Wednesday the press came, a few video crews, and he gave the interviews while reseeding the backyard, for, as he said, the lawn had been needing it for a long time: an attitude both earthy and aloof that his visitors just raved about. Thursday was devoted to paperback negotiations, which dragged on to Friday, and weren't finished until that afternoon when he had to kiss his wife and kids goodbye and fly to New York for the Bigap Literary Awards Banquet. There were rumors of talks of speculation of Hollywood feelers, but nothing came of them that night, even if, as everyone who'd read Ralph's story agreed, it was hard to imagine such a humdinger on film.

By the time he got home on Saturday all the banks were closed, it was too late to cash his checks, a fact which, combined with his mistreatment by movie moguls, left Ralph very depressed. That night he drank every bottle under the sink and abused his wife. The next day he felt ill and ashamed and turned off his phone, moping around the house in his boxer shorts; by late afternoon he managed to make her feel sorry for him. But, on Monday, he did the same thing all over again. It happened after he decided to sit down and write another humdinger; but he couldn't, the words wouldn't come, and before the evening was up he found himself in front of the football game on TV, tossing back shots of vodka, flushed and angry at the score. In the third quarter he kicked over the coffee table and started throwing things.

By Tuesday his children were totally and irreversibly screwed up. Ralph lounged in a red silk kimono, leaving the house only to catch a flight to start his reading tour, for which he jetted to many cities and college campuses and staggered full of toxins up to podiums to read his humdinger, sometimes losing his place, then teetered off to eat and drink some more and snort bags of powder up his nose and inhale clouds into his lungs and stick his penis into any orifice that would have it, discovering that there were many, an astounding number, ready and willing to be stuck into because he was the author of a humdinger, and sensitive. He spurted and spurted and spurted and didn't know where he was.

By the next weekend when a team of graduate students who were each dissecting a different aspect of his humdinger got him on the plane to Stockholm, strapped him into his seat and fled the first class cabin, all his hair had fallen out and he was in serious need of a change of clothes. But he made it through the ceremony without throwing up, thanked the King and while the bulbs flashed puffed cigars with Nobel's great-great-nephew, answering as best he could the questions about the reunification of North and South Yemen.

Ralph's death in a hotel room with a transvestite Norwegian translator is all too well known, though the truth is less sensational than the rumors—too much smoked fish lodged in the windpipe. His body was flown back on the same plane originally booked for his triumphant return, and it appears a virtual certainty that a film *will* be made, not of the humdinger, which in the week that followed the demise of the author was subjected to diverse opinions, many maintaining it was not really a humdinger after all—but the Story of Ralph. Caution, however, about the facts. Many are already lost, or forgotten. His wife has expressed no interest in cooperating with the project, and to the question, just who was Ralph, blurts: "He was an S.O.B."

Laurel and Hardy Have Sex

1.

Laurel and Hardy have sex with powder-faced ladies in polka-dot dresses. Model A Fords say: *"Toot toot!"*

2.

Laurel and Hardy have sex with their potting shed overalls undone. "Oh, Ollie! Ollie! Ollie!"

"Stan, you're the man!"

3.

Laurel and Hardy have sex with politicians and priests and parking lot attendants and—gee!—it really feels right.

4.

Laurel and Hardy have sex with sinewy beauty
and soft flesh beauty and who was that behind
the bookshelf in the Home Improvement sec-
tion?

5.

Laurel and Hardy have sex with not a penny in their potting shed overalls.

6.

Laurel and Hardy have sex during a job interview and afterwards feel that it did not go badly.

7.

Laurel and Hardy have sex with their seatbelts fastened and their tray tables secured and their seats in the upright position and it adds an extra piquancy.

8.

Laurel and Hardy have sex with an algorithm that frankly didn't see them coming and was so overwhelmed that it broke into sobs of relief and asked to be held, please, just a little longer.

9.

Laurel and Hardy have sex inside a bumping Trojan horse and the creaking wheels drown out their cries.

10.

Laurel and Hardy have sex on a breakaway ice floe with penguins in attendance under a roiling, inflamed sky.

11.

Laurel and Hardy have sex with someone in dreams who appears (so it seems) like *you*.

12.

Laurel and Hardy have sex. Model A Fords say:
"Toot toot!"

roll credits

Charles Holdefer grew up in Iowa and is a graduate of the Iowa Writers' Workshop and the Sorbonne. He currently teaches at the University of Poitiers, France.

His short fiction has appeared in many magazines, including *New England Review*, *Chicago Quarterly Review*, *North American Review*, *Los Angeles Review*, *Slice* and *Yellow Silk*. His story "The Raptor" won a Pushcart Prize.

He also writes essays and reviews which have appeared in *The Antioch Review*, *World Literature Today*, *New England Review*, *The Dactyl Review*, *The Collagist*, *l'Oeil du Spectateur*, *New York Journal of Books*, *Journal of the Short Story in English* and elsewhere.

Also by Charles Holdefer

NOVELS

Bring Me the Head of Mr. Boots (2019)
Back in the Game (2012)
The Contractor (2007)
Nice (2001)
Apology for Big Rod (1997)

STORIES

Magic Even You Can Do: By Blast (2019)
Dick Cheney in Shorts (2017)

CRITICISM

George Saunders' Pastoralia: Bookmarked (2018)